One CHRISTMAS in LUNENBURG

Written by Amy Bennet ❧ Illustrated by Don Kilby

James Lorimer & Company Ltd., Publishers

Toronto

On the day of the Christmas pageant, Rachel Whynot woke to the sound of oxen lowing. She looked out her bedroom window and saw the Whynots' neighbour, Mr. Heisler, crossing his yard. As she watched him open his barn door, she wondered if the animals inside knew that it was Christmas Eve.

Rachel, who was not quite nine, hurried to get dressed. She got into her church clothes, and pulled her hair back with two barrettes. Rachel almost always wore her hair in a ponytail that she could pull through the back of her baseball cap. But she knew it had to be barrettes for church, even if she hated them.

In the kitchen, Rachel's six-year-old brother Nathan was already having breakfast. He was wearing her favourite ball cap.

"Hey," Rachel said. "That's mine! Give it back." She spoke both out loud and in sign language. Nathan was born with Down's syndrome, and some things, like speaking, took him a long time to learn.

Nathan signed the word "no," then, giggling, turned the cap backwards and flicked a piece of cereal at his sister.

Rachel poured herself some cereal and said, signing with her hands, "You'd better hurry up and get ready for church."

Nathan signed two words.

"That's right," she nodded, "Christmas story. We're going to be in the pageant today."

Nathan made the sign for Santa by stroking his chin as though he had a long beard.

"Yes, Santa's coming, but not until after the pageant. He'll come tonight when we're asleep," Rachel answered. "Now get moving or we'll be late!"

For Jeff, Henry and Lucy and our friends, the real Rachel and Nathan. — A.B.

For Nancy, who makes our home a happy one. — D.K.

Text copyright © 2004 Amy Bennet
Illustrations copyright © 2004 Don Kilby

James Lorimer & Company Ltd. acknowledges the support of the Ontario Arts Council. We acknowledge the support of the Government of Canada through the Book Publishing Industry Development Program (BPIDP) for our publishing activities. We acknowledge the support of the Canada Council for the Arts for our publishing program. We acknowledge the support of the Government of Ontario through the Ontario Media Development Corporation's Ontario Book Initiative.

Library and Archives Canada Cataloguing in Publication

Bennet, A. B. (Amy Brook), 1964-
    One Christmas in Lunenburg / written by Amy Bennet ; illustrated by Don Kilby.

ISBN 1-55028-868-7
    1. Lunenburg (N.S.)—Juvenile fiction.
2. Christmas stories, Canadian (English) I. Kilby, Don II. Title.

PS8603.E559O54 2004 jC813'.6   C2004-904300-5

James Lorimer & Company Ltd., Publishers
35 Britain Street
Toronto, Ontario
M5A 1R7
www.lorimer.ca

Distributed in the U.S. by:
Orca Book Publishers
P.O. Box 468 Custer, WA
USA 98240-046

Printed and bound in China

The Canada Council | Le Conseil des Arts
for the Arts | du Canada

ONTARIO ARTS COUNCIL
CONSEIL DES ARTS DE L'ONTARIO

Rachel knew then that what she had seen and heard this Christmas Eve was the best true story of all, and that someday she would pass this one on.

"Thanks, Nathan," she said.

Nathan took one of Mr. Heisler's hands and one of Rachel's. They headed back across the barnyard, toward the warmth of their beds and the waiting wonder of Christmas Day.

In the dim light, Rachel could see her brother leaning in close to one of the oxen.

"Careful, son," said Mr. Heisler. "Go easy."

Nathan's head was tilted as if he was listening to a whisper. His lips were moving. The ox rose to its feet, and Nathan turned back toward the door.

And then Rachel heard a sound she had never heard before, Nathan saying her name.

"Ra–chel…" Nathan took a deep breath before he continued speaking. "True," he said without signing. "True."

Rachel woke with a start. At first she thought it must be early morning — Christmas Day! But then she heard the sound of church bells and saw the stars in the dark sky through her window. All along the South Shore church bells were chiming for their midnight service. It was midnight on Christmas Eve.

Rachel slipped out of bed and into Nathan's room.

"Nathan," she whispered, shaking her brother gently. "Come with me."

Nathan rubbed his sleepy eyes. He signed the word "Santa."

"He won't get to Lunenburg until later," Rachel said. "Let's go see the animals. Quiet, though. We have to tiptoe."

Rachel and Nathan crept down the back stairs and found their boots and jackets. After easing the door shut behind them, they ran across the field to Mr. Heisler's barn. Suddenly, a screen door banged shut, making them jump. Rachel frantically looked around for somewhere to hide, but it was too late. They were caught in the beam of Mr. Heisler's flashlight.

"Well, look here …" Mr. Heisler said, "Shouldn't you young ones be in bed at this hour?"

Rachel stared down at the snow. She swallowed hard, trying not to cry.

"Aw, come now, my girl," said Mr. Heisler, walking over and patting her shoulder. "I think I know what you're doing in the barnyard tonight."

Rachel felt herself start to breathe again.

"Let's go take a look," the old man said.

They stood for a moment outside the barn door. Now that she was here, and her question would finally be answered, Rachel wanted to turn and run away, but she couldn't make her feet move. As Nathan reached for the latch, Rachel put out a hand to stop him, but he brushed her away. He lifted the latch, pulled open the big door, and slipped inside.

Later that night, after Rachel and Nathan had hung up their stockings, they put on their pajamas and crawled into their beds. Rachel pulled her heavy quilt up under her chin and listened.

She heard her parents talking softly downstairs.

She heard Nathan breathing in the next room, where he was already fast asleep.

She could even hear the bells on Mr. Heisler's oxen jangling faintly as they settled into their straw for the night.

Rachel closed her eyes and began to count silently, hoping by the time she got to ninety-nine it would be Christmas morning.

great-great-grandfather told it..."

"But is it true?" Rachel asked again. "Do they really speak in words, like us? I thought maybe it could be a true story, since it's been around for so long."

And, she thought to herself, *it's about Jesus and that makes it holy.*

"Maybe it's one of those things that we're not supposed to know for sure," Rachel's father said as they pulled up to the church. "Maybe we're just supposed to imagine it could be true."

After the pageant ended and the parents had finished clapping, Rachel turned to her Sunday school teacher, tugging on her sleeve. "Miss Tanner," Rachel said. "Can you tell me if it's true? Our story about the animals?"

Miss Tanner smiled. "I'd like to think it might be true. But maybe the most important thing is that it's a story we all love to hear." Then she called out, "Okay, kids. Time to change out of our costumes!" and disappeared behind the stage.

Rachel felt like she hadn't been given much of an answer at all.

"You were a great sheep, Nathan," Rachel said to her brother as they changed out of their costumes.

Nathan signed the words, "good story."

Rachel looked at her brother, still wearing half of his sheep outfit. "Yeah, it's a good story," she agreed. "Maybe that's all it is."

Nathan made two signs.

Rachel laughed. "Santa later. Don't worry, he's coming!"

On the way to church, the Whynots drove past Mr. Heisler's field. "Mum," Rachel said from the back seat, "is the story about the animals true?"

"Which story?" her mother asked.

"The pageant story — about how animals all over the world speak out loud at midnight on Christmas Eve to celebrate the birth of Jesus."

"It's a nice one, isn't it?" her mother said. "You know, my father used to tell it every year, and his father told it, and even your

After supper, the family took a drive through Lunenburg. Holiday lights sparkled on the crisp snow, and the streets seemed quietly beautiful. Nathan pointed out the window at all the Christmas trees in the town square. "Presents coming?" he signed.

"Soon!" Rachel said. "Only one more sleep!"

"Rachel present coming," Nathan signed.

"You're giving me a gift?"

Nathan stuck out his tongue. "No," he signed. Then he grabbed Rachel's ball cap and put it on backwards.

Rachel punched his arm lightly. "You're such a joker!"

As they waited for the hours to pass until they could hang their stockings, Rachel and Nathan went sledding on Mr. Heisler's hill. It was getting close to suppertime when Rachel saw their neighbour coming out of his barn. "Hey, Mr. Heisler, can I ask you something?" Rachel called out.

"Sure, my girl, ask away," Mr. Heisler said, pushing his wool cap back.

"I was wondering," Rachel said, "do you know if our pageant story is true? Can all the animals talk out loud at midnight on Christmas Eve?"

Beside her, Nathan made the sign for "true."

Mr. Heisler chuckled. "The only words I've ever heard from my animals are 'give me more food,'" he said, "And they usually say that with a cackle or a moo, not in real words."

"Oh, okay." Rachel said, trying to smile. If Mr. Heisler hadn't heard the animals talk, then maybe it never really happened. He'd spent his whole life around animals. "Well, merry Christmas," she said.

"Merry Christmas," replied Mr. Heisler.

Rachel picked up her sled and followed Nathan back up the hill.